First published in 1986 by Hutchinson Children's Books Ltd
An imprint of Century Hutchinson Ltd
Brookmount House, 62-65 Chandos Place, Covent Garden, London WC2N 4NW

Century Hutchinson Publishing Group (Australia) Pty Ltd
16-22 Church Street, Hawthorn, Melbourne, Victoria 3122

Century Hutchinson Group (NZ) Ltd
32-34 View Road, PO Box 40-086, Glenfield, Auckland 10

Century Hutchinson Group (SA) Pty Ltd
PO Box 337, Bergvlei 2012, South Africa

Designed by Sarah Harwood
Edited by Sarah Ware

Set in Stymie Light, by The Keystroke Mill
Printed and bound in Italy

British Library Cataloguing in Publication Data
Hunt, Roderick, *1939-*
Mole wins a prize
I. Title   II. Gordon, Mike
823'.914[J]   PZ7

ISBN 0 09 167520 0

MOLE
wins a
prize

Written by Rod Hunt
Illustrated by Mike Gordon

Hutchinson
London   Melbourne   Auckland   Johannesburg

'Has anyone seen Mole?' asked Stoat. 'I passed her last night. She said she'd meet me here today and tell me something really important.'

'She said the same to me,' put in Fox.

'Me too,' said Frog. 'It was something she'd overheard. It sounded serious.'

At that moment a little patch of earth near Fox began to move and Mole popped up out of the ground. 'Sorry I'm late,' she said, shaking the dirt from her fur, 'but I came by tunnel. I didn't want to be seen.'

'What have you got to tell us?' asked Fox anxiously.

Mole looked round about cautiously, then whispered, 'I heard the animals of North Wood talking last night. They want to stop us using the Hollow. They say we've no right to be there.'

'But we've always used the Hollow,' said Stoat. 'Badger loves going there.'

Just then Rabbit raced into the clearing.
She crashed into Mole, knocking her over,
and skidded to a stop in front of Fox.

'I say, Rabbit!' protested Mole. 'Do be
careful. You might have hurt me.'

'What's the hurry, Rabbit?' asked Fox. 'Is
something wrong?'

'Oh listen, everyone,' panted Rabbit. 'Badger is about to have a fight. You must come at once. We've got to stop him.'

'A fight!' exclaimed Frog. 'It's hard to imagine Badger wanting a fight with anyone.'

'Don't hang about,' said Rabbit. 'Run!'

Mole, Stoat, Fox and Frog hurried after
Rabbit. Soon they came to the part of the
wood known as the Hollow. There they
found Badger, his grey whiskers bristling
with anger. He stood glaring at another
much younger badger, who looked very
cross indeed.

'We've always used the Hollow,' said Badger. 'It belongs to us.'

'Oh no it doesn't,' argued the young badger. 'You animals from South Wood have no right to be here. It belongs to us.'

'How dare you!' growled Badger, giving the young badger a shove. It certainly looked as if the two were about to fight.

'Oh!' cried Mole. 'We must stop them.' Suddenly something swooped down between the badgers with a fluttering and flapping of wings. Owl had arrived to stop the fight.

'I'm ashamed of you both,' said Owl sternly. 'You can't settle things by fighting. Why don't you all share the Hollow?'

Badger looked horrified. 'But there isn't room for all of us,' he said. 'No, we've got to find a way of deciding who it belongs to.'

Mole suddenly had an idea, but she was far too shy to say it out loud. Instead she whispered it to Stoat, who told the others.

'We could have a contest,' said Stoat, 'to decide who will own the Hollow.'

'What sort of contest?' asked Owl.

'A talent contest,' said Stoat, 'between the animals of North Wood and South Wood. Each side can put on a show with dancing, singing and tricks. Owl will be the judge and the prize will be the Hollow.'

'That's a jolly good idea,' said the young badger.

All the animals agreed that it was
excellent, but Stoat didn't tell them it was
Mole's own idea.

Frog got excited. 'I can do some tricks,'
he said, doing a backward somersault.

Owl said that the contest would be held
the next day at the big tree stump.

Later that day, Badger called together the animals of South Wood and told them about the contest. 'I want each one of you to tell me what you can do,' he said.

'I can tap dance,' said Hedgehog.

'I can juggle,' said Squirrel.

Rabbit said she could do some magic. Frog wanted to do somersaults. Fox said she could do funny voices. Badger agreed to sing and Stoat said he'd tell a story.

'How about you, Mole?' asked Badger. 'You haven't said what you can do.'

Mole felt a funny sick feeling in her tummy.
Even though the talent contest was her
idea, she didn't think she'd have to take
part in it. She was far too shy for that.

'Oh . . . oh!' she stammered. 'I couldn't
do anything in front of the other animals.'

'Well, really!' said Badger, crossly. 'We're willing to have a go. Why aren't you?'

'I really couldn't,' said Mole. 'Sorry.'

Without another word, she popped down her tunnel and ran as far as it would go, then lay down miserably in the dark.

'I'm not clever like the others,' thought Mole. 'They can dance and sing. That's why the talent contest is a good idea. But even if I could do something I'd be too shy.'

Suddenly Mole heard voices. Some children were having a picnic just above her tunnel.

She was just about to run back along it
when something funny made her stop and
listen. She heard what the children said
and laughed so much that she forgot to be
miserable.

Mole was still laughing long after the
children had gone home.

The next day was the talent contest. The animals gathered round the big tree stump and Owl judged each act in turn.

By the end of the contest the South Wood team began to lose. If Stoat won the last act, they would win the contest. But where was he?

Mole crept up and found Stoat hiding. 'I can't do it,' he said, shaking with fear.

Mole knew she had to think of something quickly. There was one thing, perhaps, if only she dared. She felt her cheeks burn and her claws tremble, but she knew she must do it.

To everyone's surprise, Mole climbed on
to the tree stump.

'I say, I say,' she began, shyly. 'Why are
goldfish orange? Because the water makes
them rusty!' Everyone laughed.

'Why can't ducks fly upside down?
Because they would quack up!' Everyone
laughed again.

Mole soon forgot that she was shy and went on.

'When do badgers have eight feet? When there are two of them!' The animals were helpless with laughter.

When they had calmed down they all agreed that Mole's act was the best and Owl awarded her top marks.

Thanks to Mole the animals of South Wood
won the Hollow.

The animals of North Wood were good
sports. 'It was a fair contest,' they said.

'Your surprise act made us win, Mole,'
said Badger. 'Wherever did you find all
your jokes?'

'I overheard some children telling them,' said Mole, glowing with pleasure.

'Well, I haven't laughed so much for ages,' said Owl. 'Mole should get a special prize.'

'Oh, I've got the best prize of all,' said Mole. 'I've learned not to be shy anymore.'